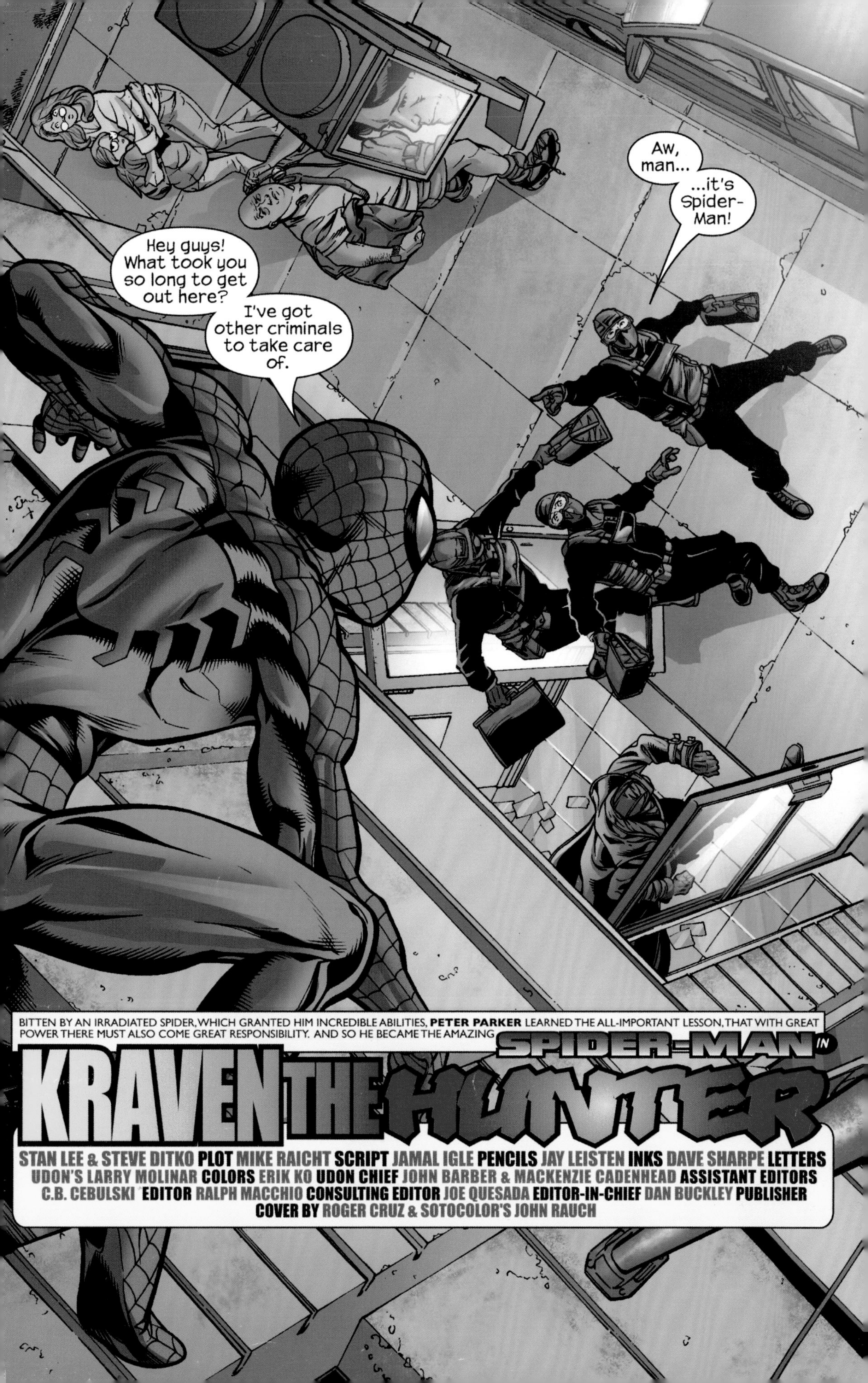

Hey guys! What took you so long to get out here?
I've got other criminals to take care of.
Aw, man...
...it's Spider-Man!
BITTEN BY AN IRRADIATED SPIDER, WHICH GRANTED HIM INCREDIBLE ABILITIES, PETER PARKER LEARNED THE ALL-IMPORTANT LESSON, THAT WITH GREAT POWER THERE MUST ALSO COME GREAT RESPONSIBILITY. AND SO HE BECAME THE AMAZING SPIDER-MAN IN
KRAVEN THE HUNTER
STAN LEE & STEVE DITKO PLOT MIKE RAICHT SCRIPT JAMAL IGLE PENCILS JAY LEISTEN INKS DAVE SHARPE LETTERS
UDON'S LARRY MOLINAR COLORS ERIK KO UDON CHIEF JOHN BARBER & MACKENZIE CADENHEAD ASSISTANT EDITORS
C.B. CEBULSKI EDITOR RALPH MACCHIO CONSULTING EDITOR JOE QUESADA EDITOR-IN-CHIEF DAN BUCKLEY PUBLISHER
COVER BY ROGER CRUZ & SOTOCOLOR'S JOHN RAUCH

VISIT US AT
www.abdopub.com

Spotlight, a division of ABDO Publishing Company Inc., is the school and library distributor of the Marvel Entertainment books.

Library bound edition © 2006

Printed in the United States of America, North Mankato, Minnesota.

012005
022012

Library of Congress Cataloging-in-Publication Data

Kraven The Hunter

ISBN 1-59961-009-4   (Reinforced Library Bound Edition)

All Spotlight books are reinforced library binding and manufactured in the United States of America

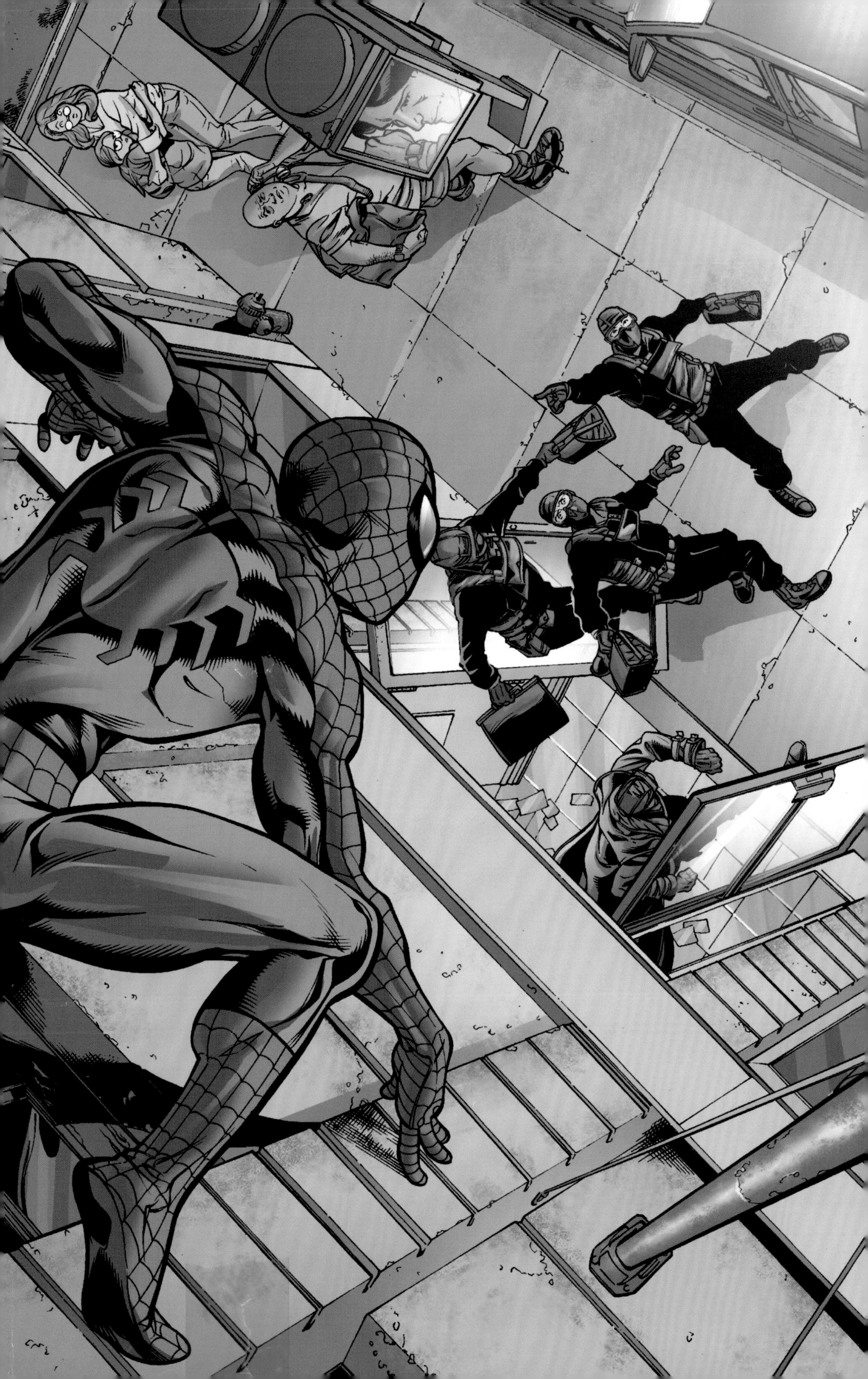

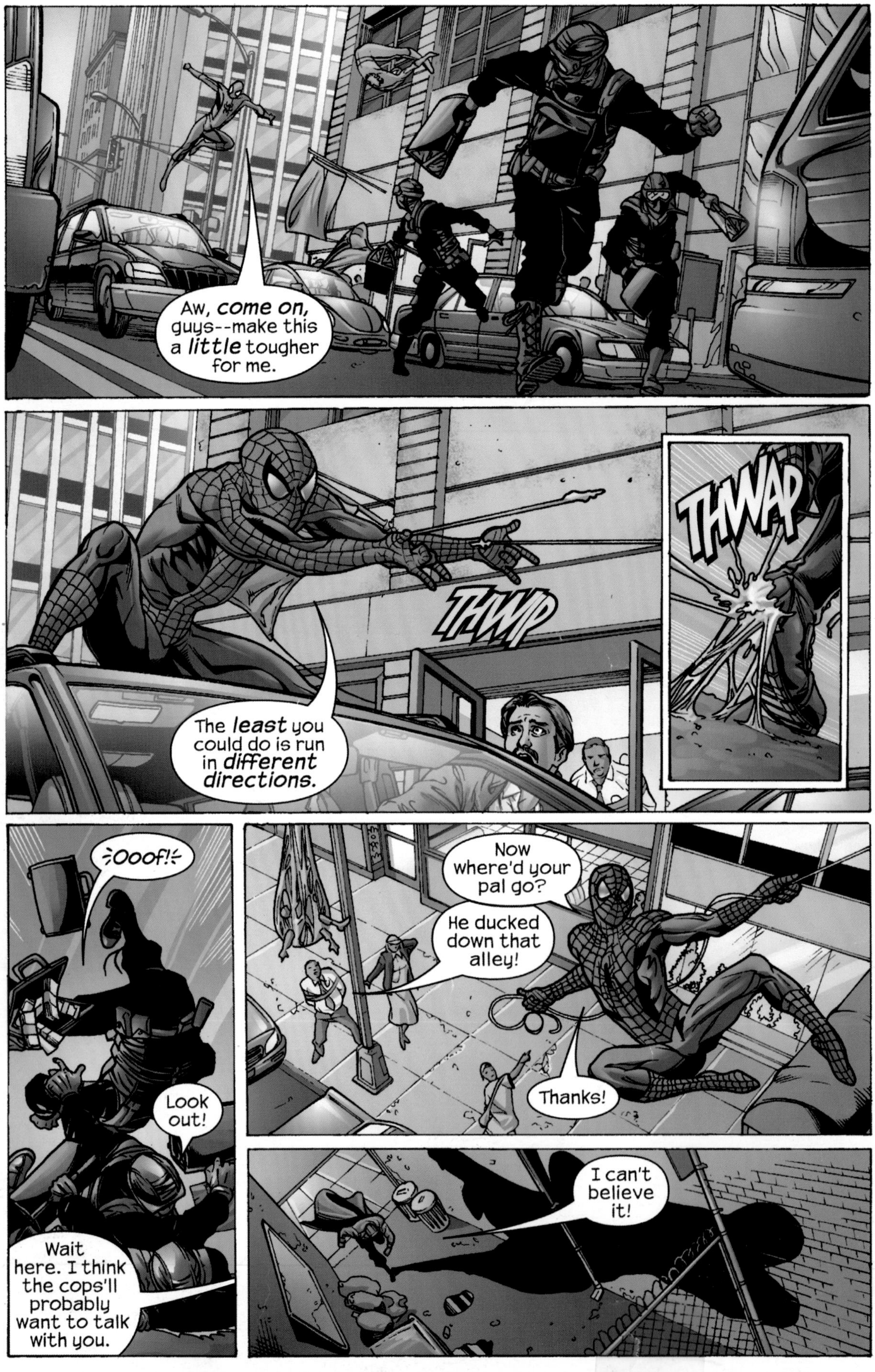

Aw, come on, guys--make this a little tougher for me.
THWAP
THWIP
The least you could do is run in different directions.
Ooof!
Look out!
Wait here. I think the cops'll probably want to talk with you.
Now where'd your pal go?
He ducked down that alley!
Thanks!
I can't believe it!

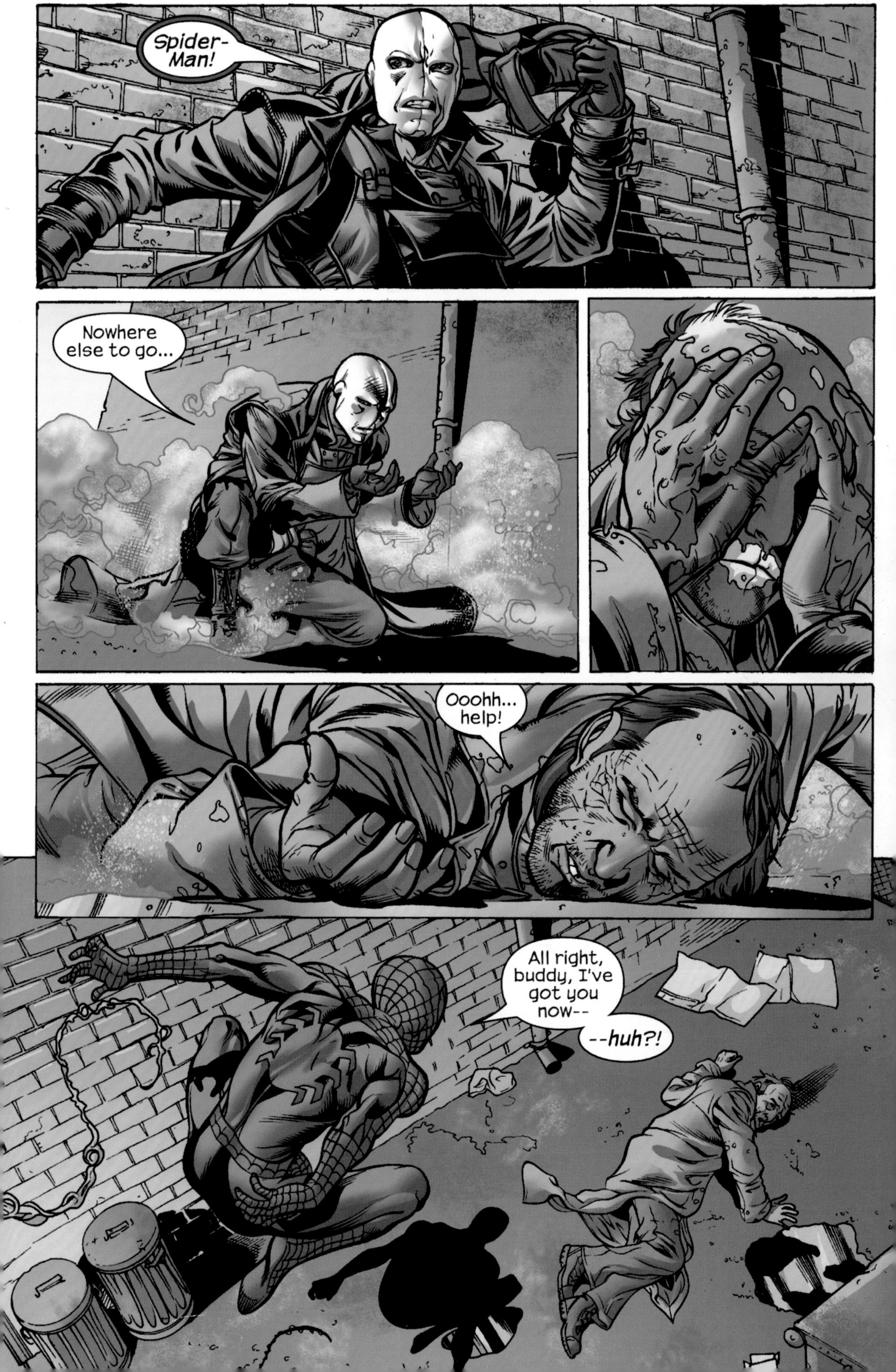
Spider-Man!
Nowhere else to go...
Ooohh... help!
All right, buddy, I've got you now--
--huh?!

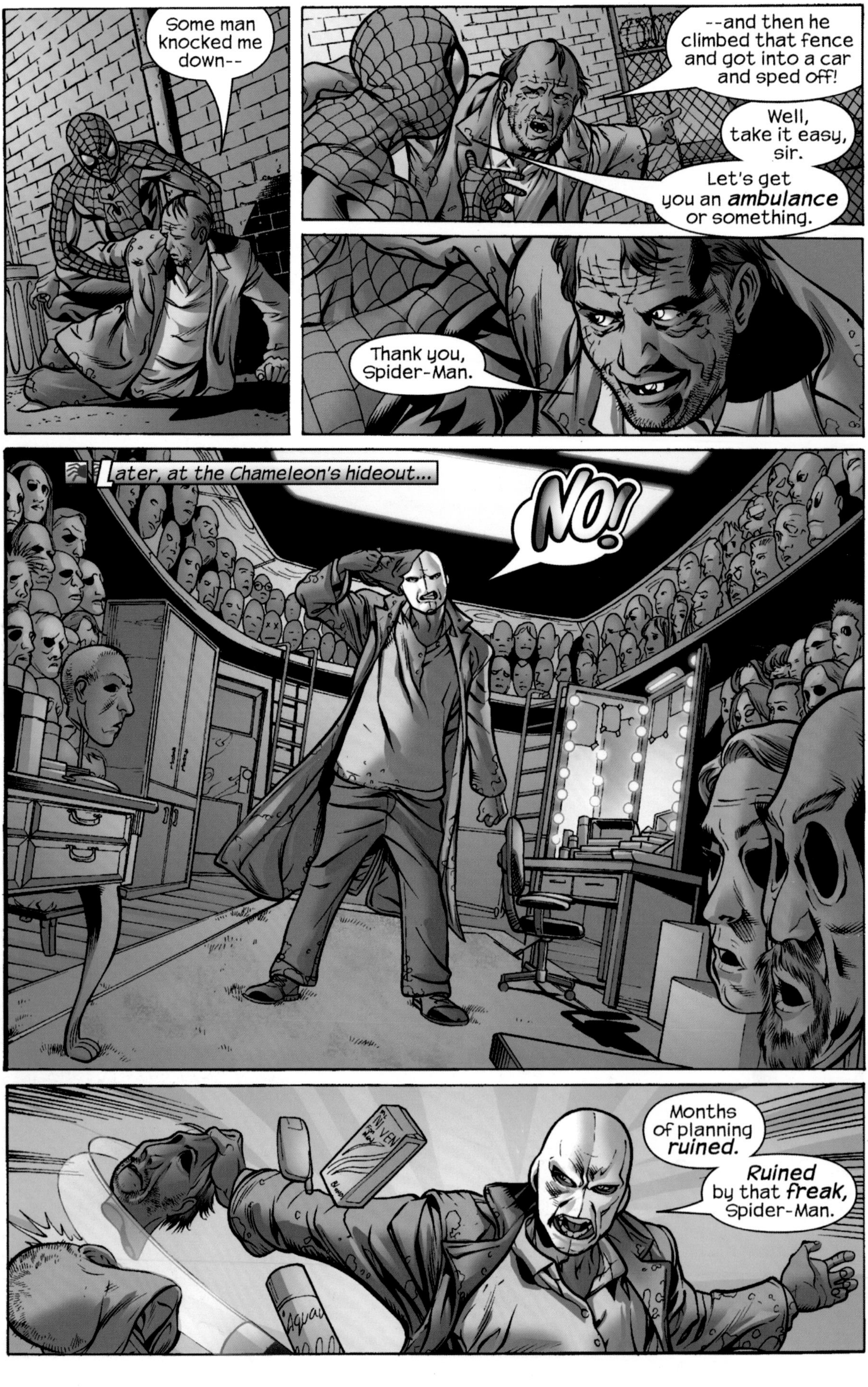
Some man knocked me down--
--and then he climbed that fence and got into a car and sped off!
Well, take it easy, sir.
Let's get you an *ambulance* or something.
Thank you, Spider-Man.
Later, at the Chameleon's hideout...
NO!
Months of planning *ruined.*
Ruined by that *freak,* Spider-Man.

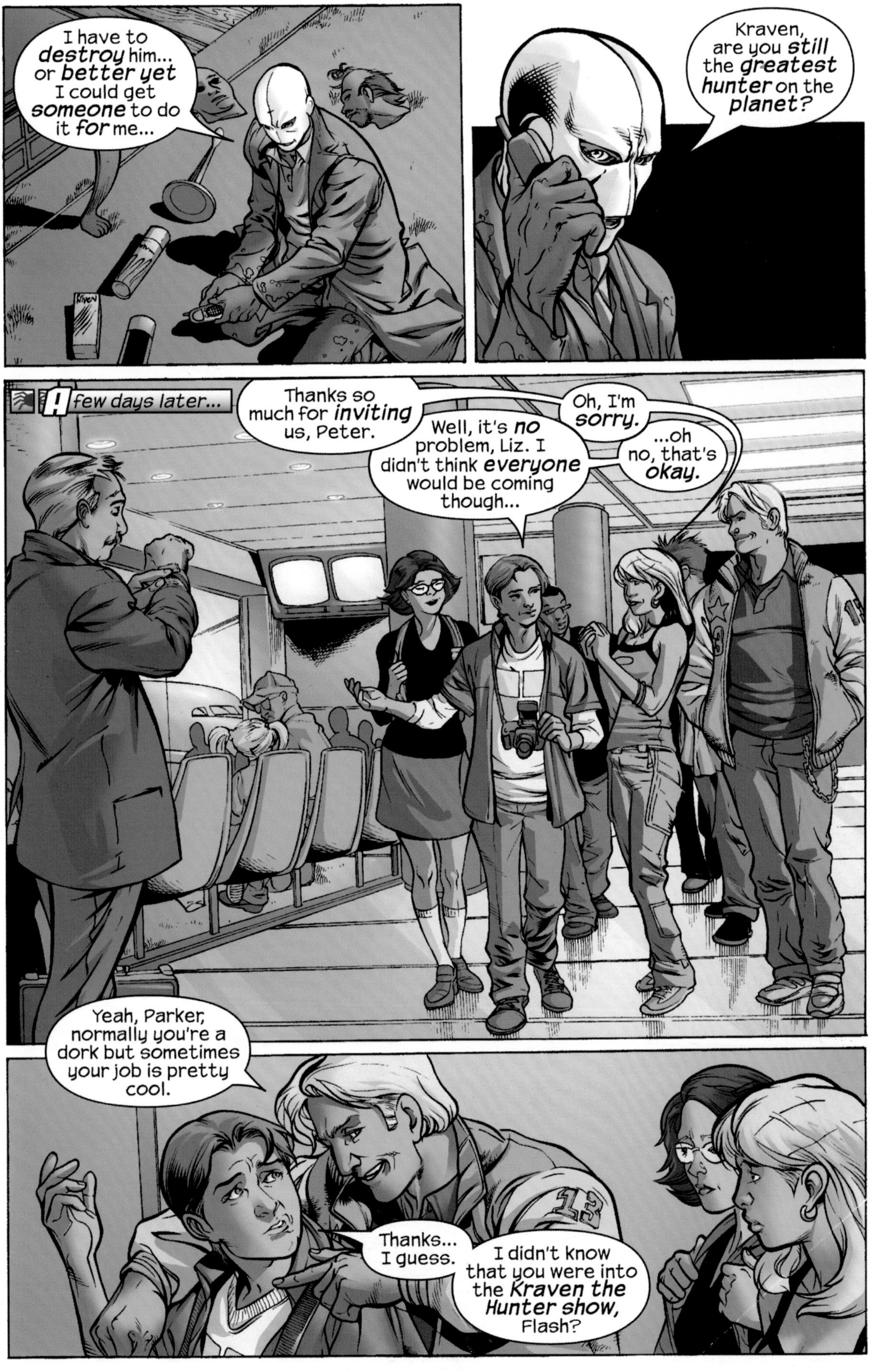
I have to destroy him... or better yet I could get someone to do it for me...
Kraven, are you still the greatest hunter on the planet?
A few days later...
Thanks so much for inviting us, Peter.
Well, it's no problem, Liz. I didn't think everyone would be coming though...
Oh, I'm sorry.
...oh no, that's okay.
Yeah, Parker, normally you're a dork but sometimes your job is pretty cool.
Thanks... I guess.
I didn't know that you were into the Kraven the Hunter show, Flash?

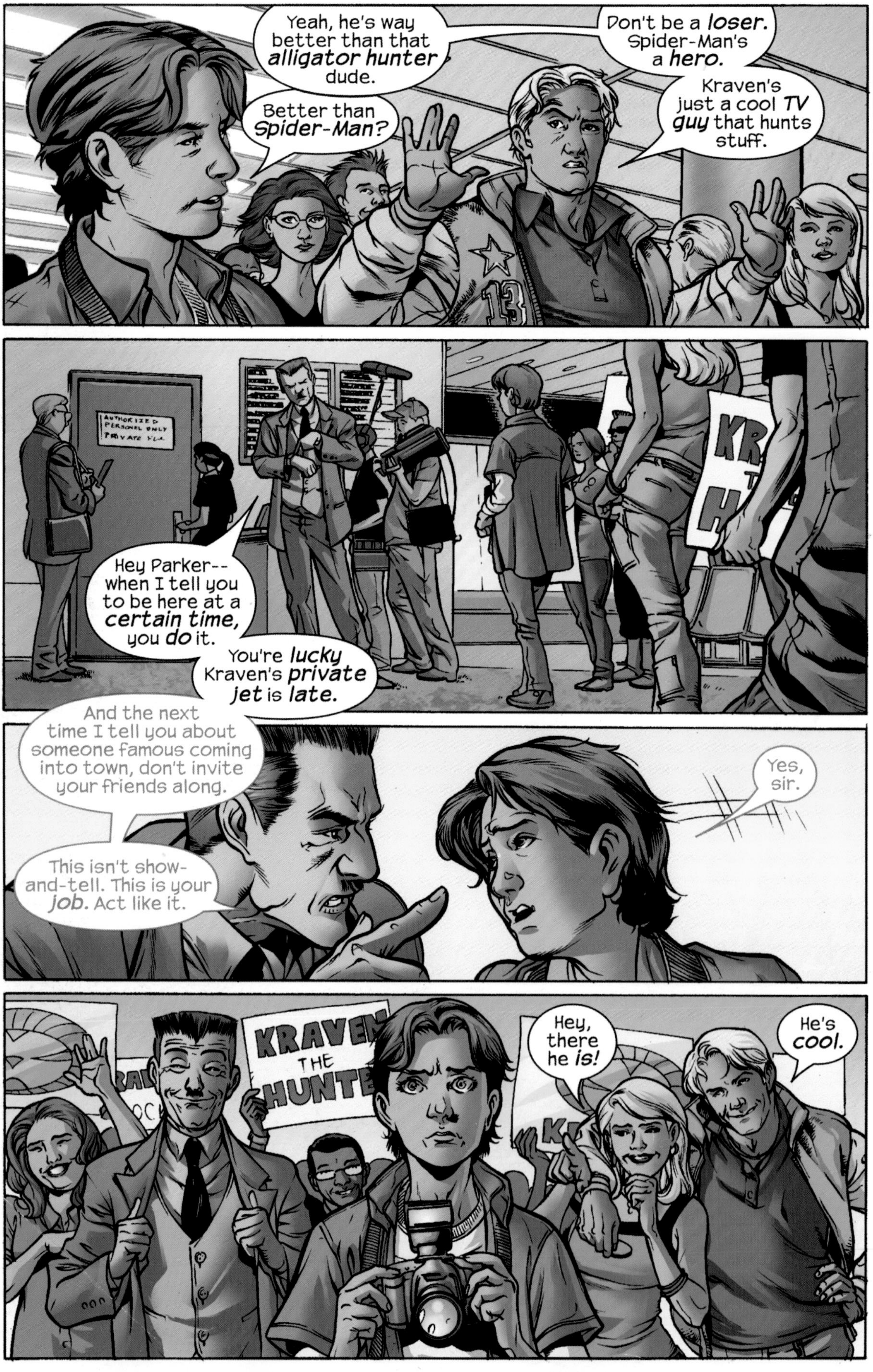
Yeah, he's way better than that alligator hunter dude.
Better than Spider-Man?
Don't be a loser. Spider-Man's a hero.
Kraven's just a cool TV guy that hunts stuff.
Hey Parker-- when I tell you to be here at a certain time, you do it.
You're lucky Kraven's private jet is late.
And the next time I tell you about someone famous coming into town, don't invite your friends along.
This isn't show-and-tell. This is your job. Act like it.
Yes, sir.
KRAVEN THE HUNTE
Hey, there he is!
He's cool.

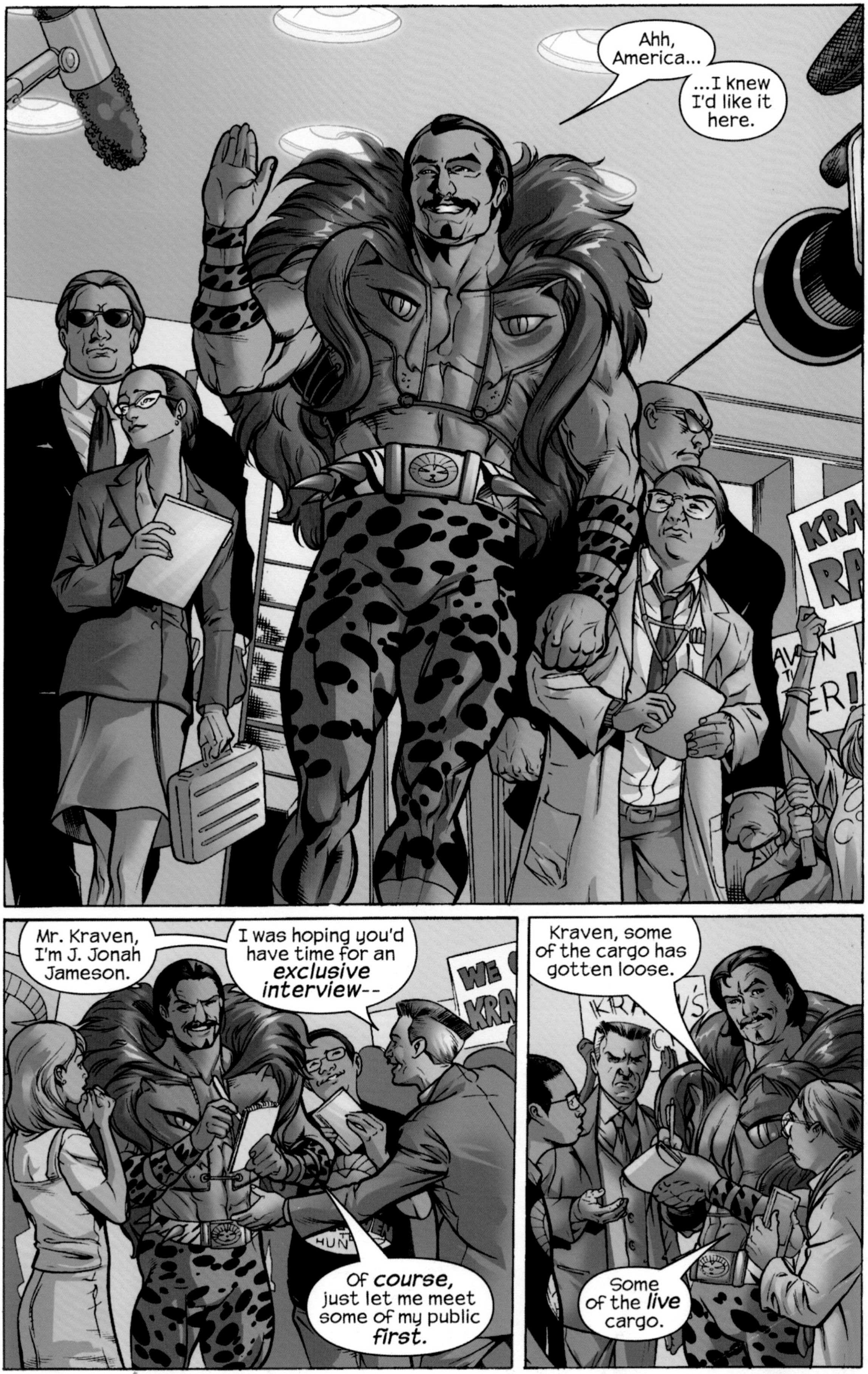
Ahh, America...
...I knew I'd like it here.
Mr. Kraven, I'm J. Jonah Jameson.
I was hoping you'd have time for an *exclusive interview*--
Of *course,* just let me meet some of my public *first.*
Kraven, some of the cargo has gotten loose.
Some of the *live* cargo.

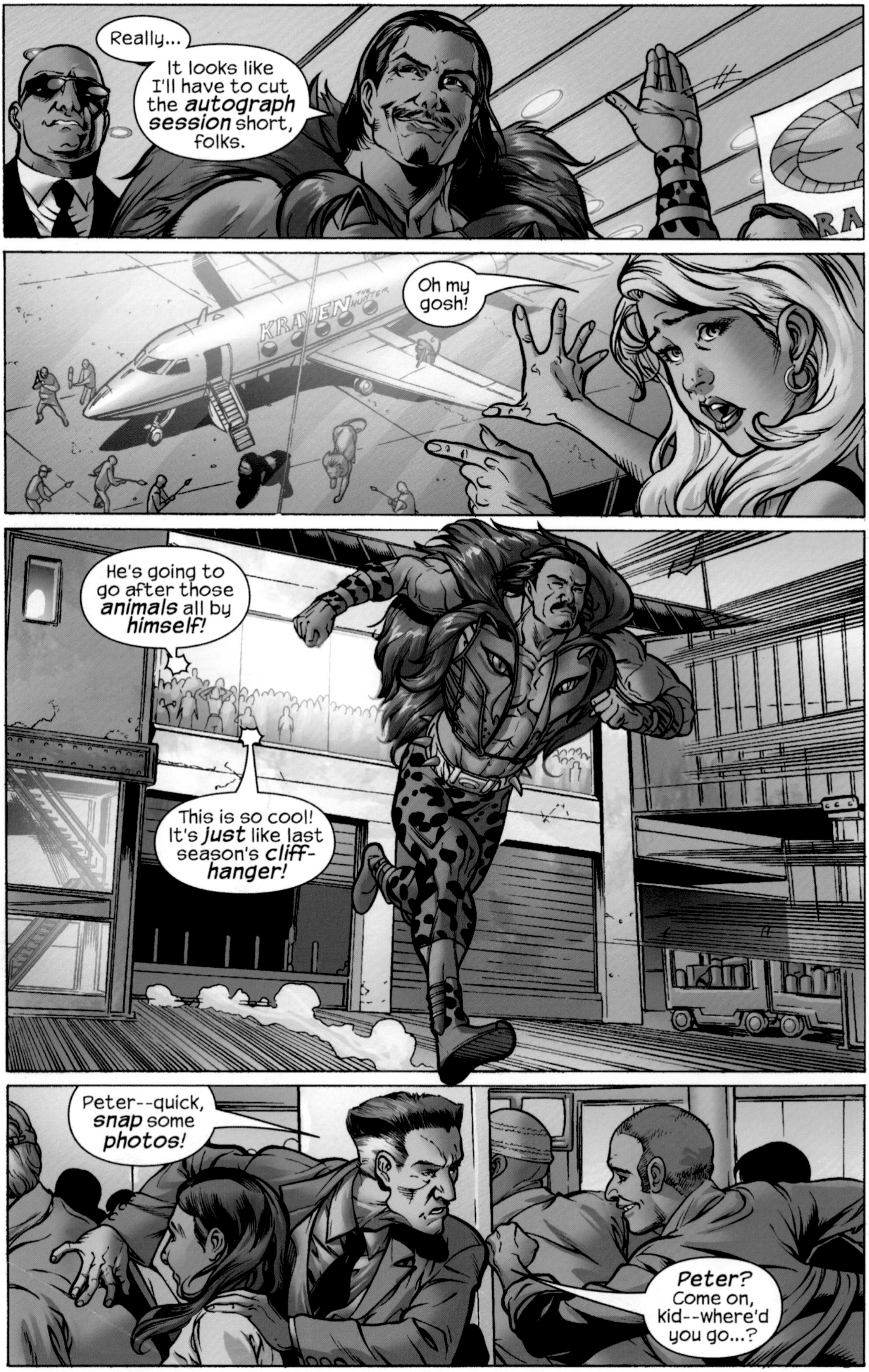
Really...
It looks like I'll have to cut the autograph session short, folks.
Oh my gosh!
KRAVEN THE HUNTER
He's going to go after those animals all by himself!
This is so cool! It's just like last season's cliff-hanger!
Peter--quick, snap some photos!
Peter? Come on, kid--where'd you go...?

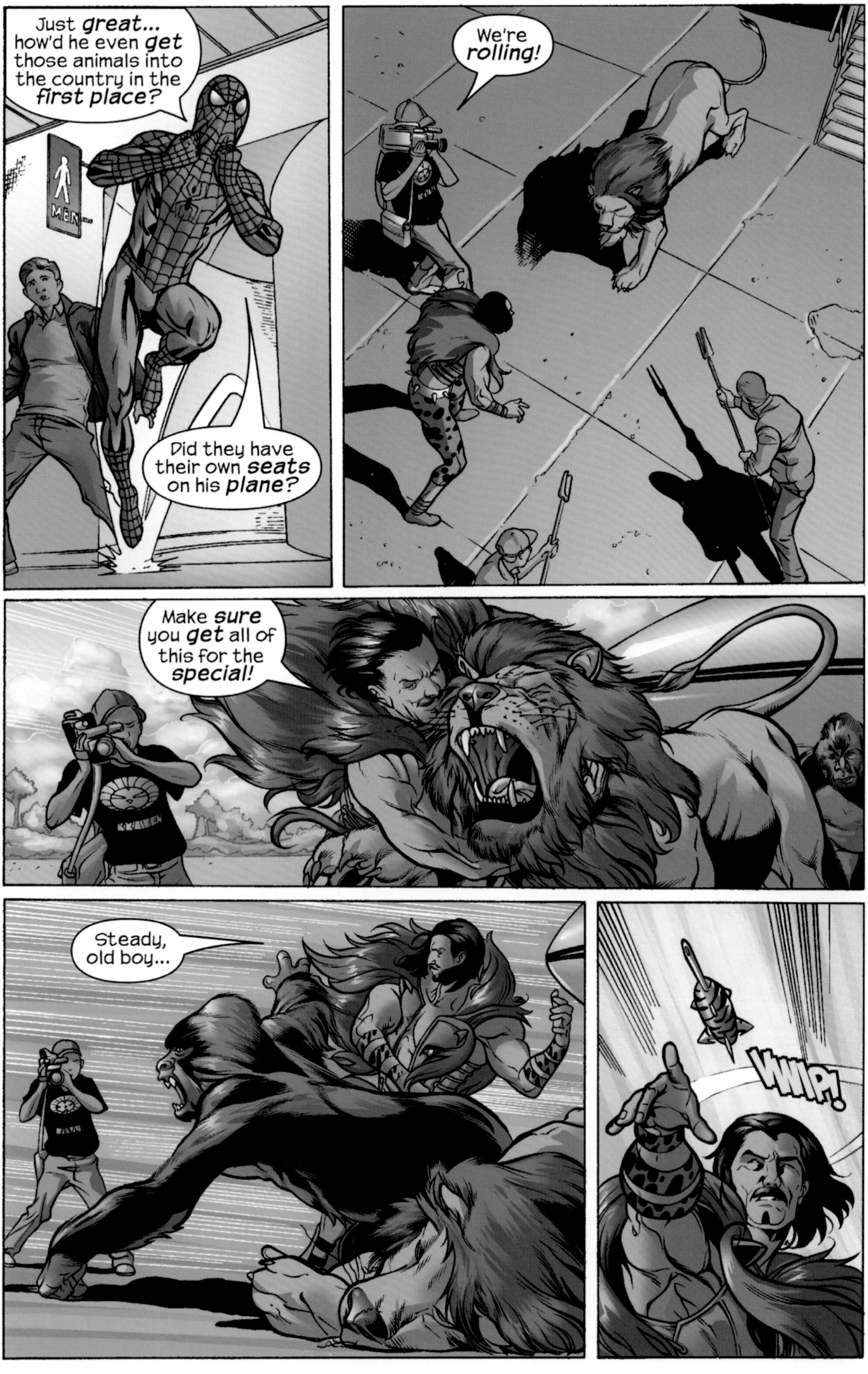
Just great... how'd he even get those animals into the country in the first place?
MEN
Did they have their own seats on his plane?
We're rolling!
Make sure you get all of this for the special!
Steady, old boy...
WHIP!

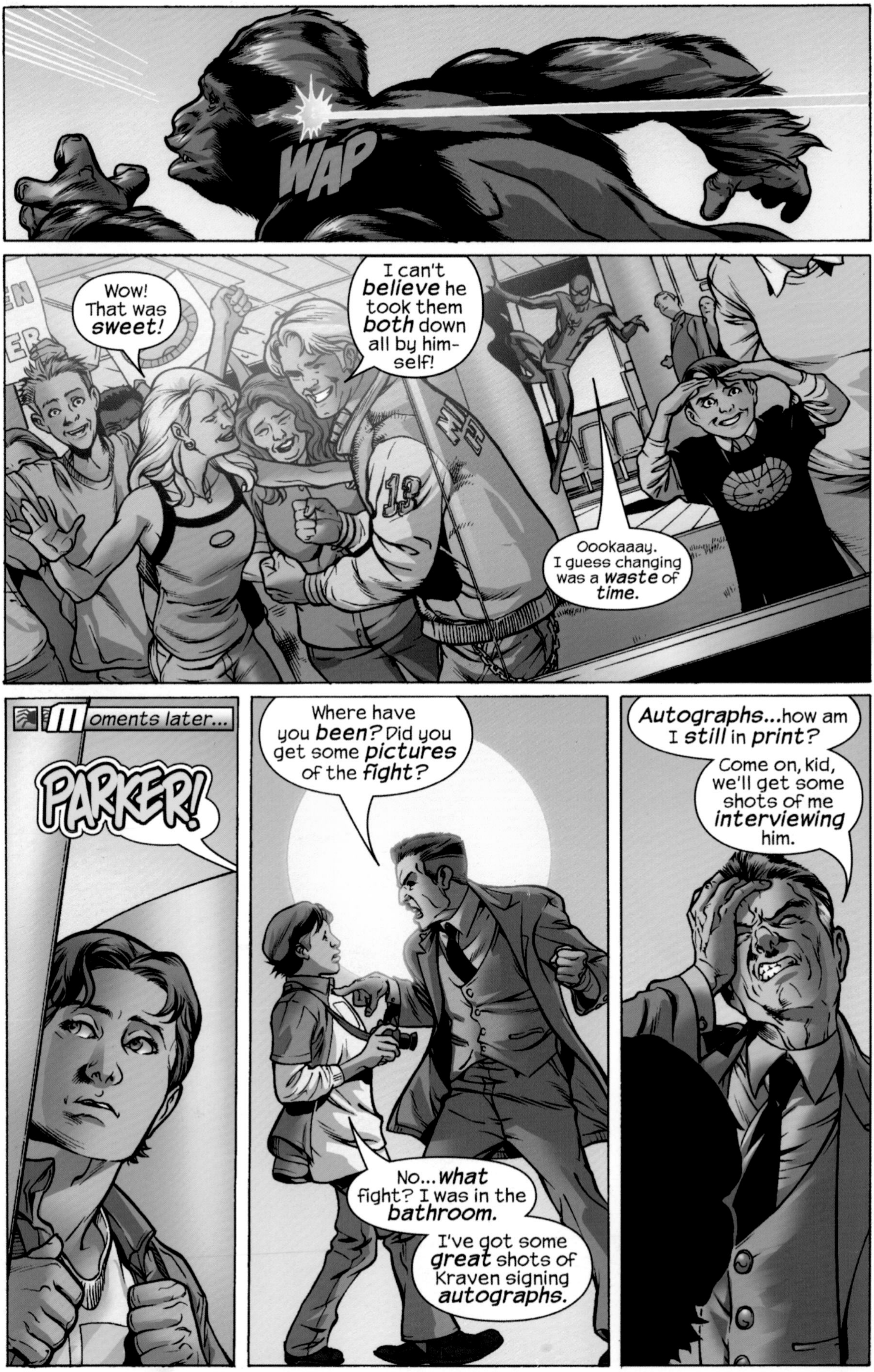
WAP
Wow! That was sweet!
I can't believe he took them both down all by him-self!
Oookaaay. I guess changing was a waste of time.
Moments later...
PARKER!
Where have you been? Did you get some pictures of the fight?
No...what fight? I was in the bathroom.
I've got some great shots of Kraven signing autographs.
Autographs...how am I still in print?
Come on, kid, we'll get some shots of me interviewing him.

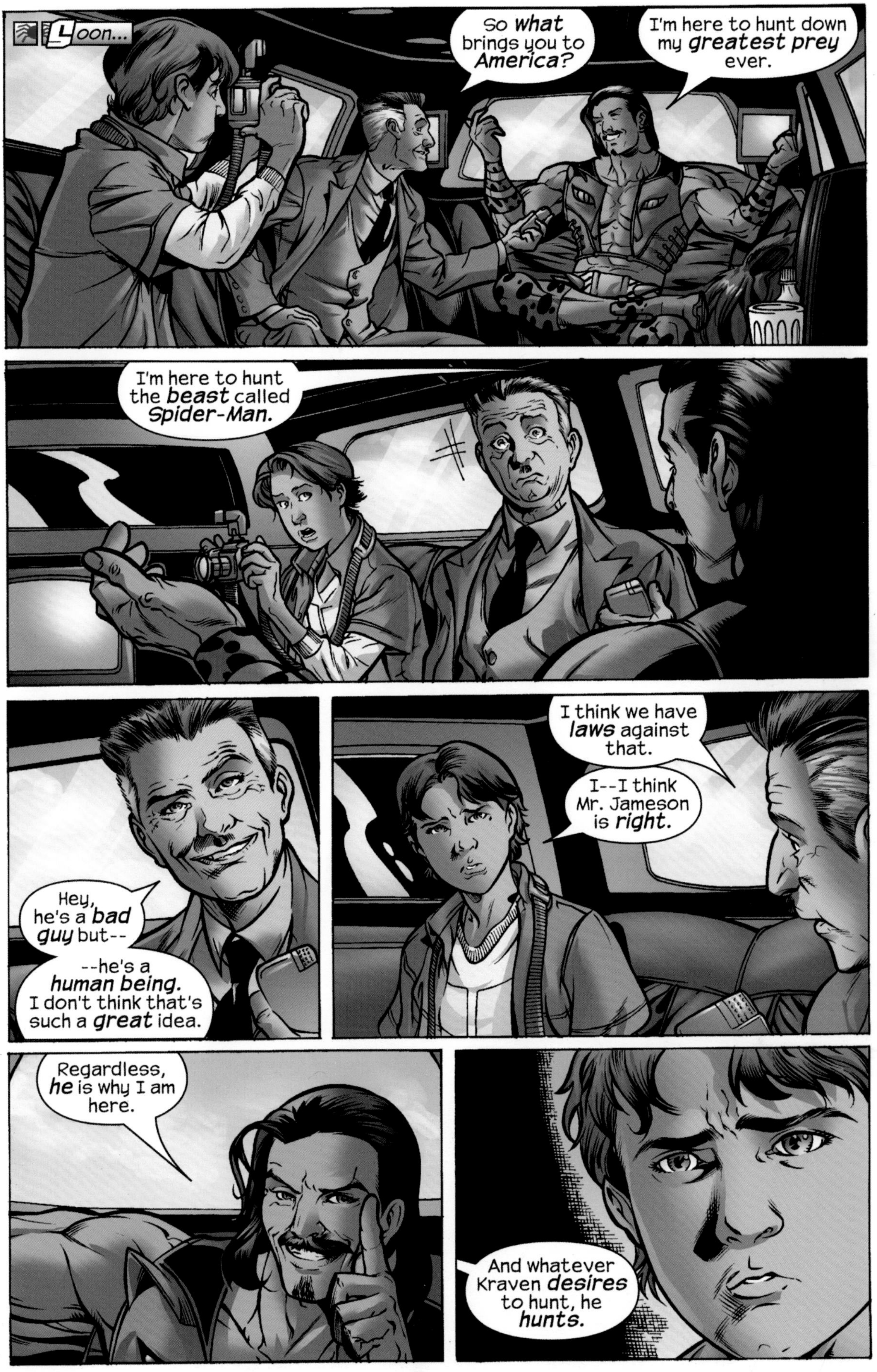
Soon...
So what brings you to America?
I'm here to hunt down my greatest prey ever.
I'm here to hunt the beast called Spider-Man.
Hey, he's a bad guy but--
--he's a human being. I don't think that's such a great idea.
I think we have laws against that.
I--I think Mr. Jameson is right.
Regardless, he is why I am here.
And whatever Kraven desires to hunt, he hunts.

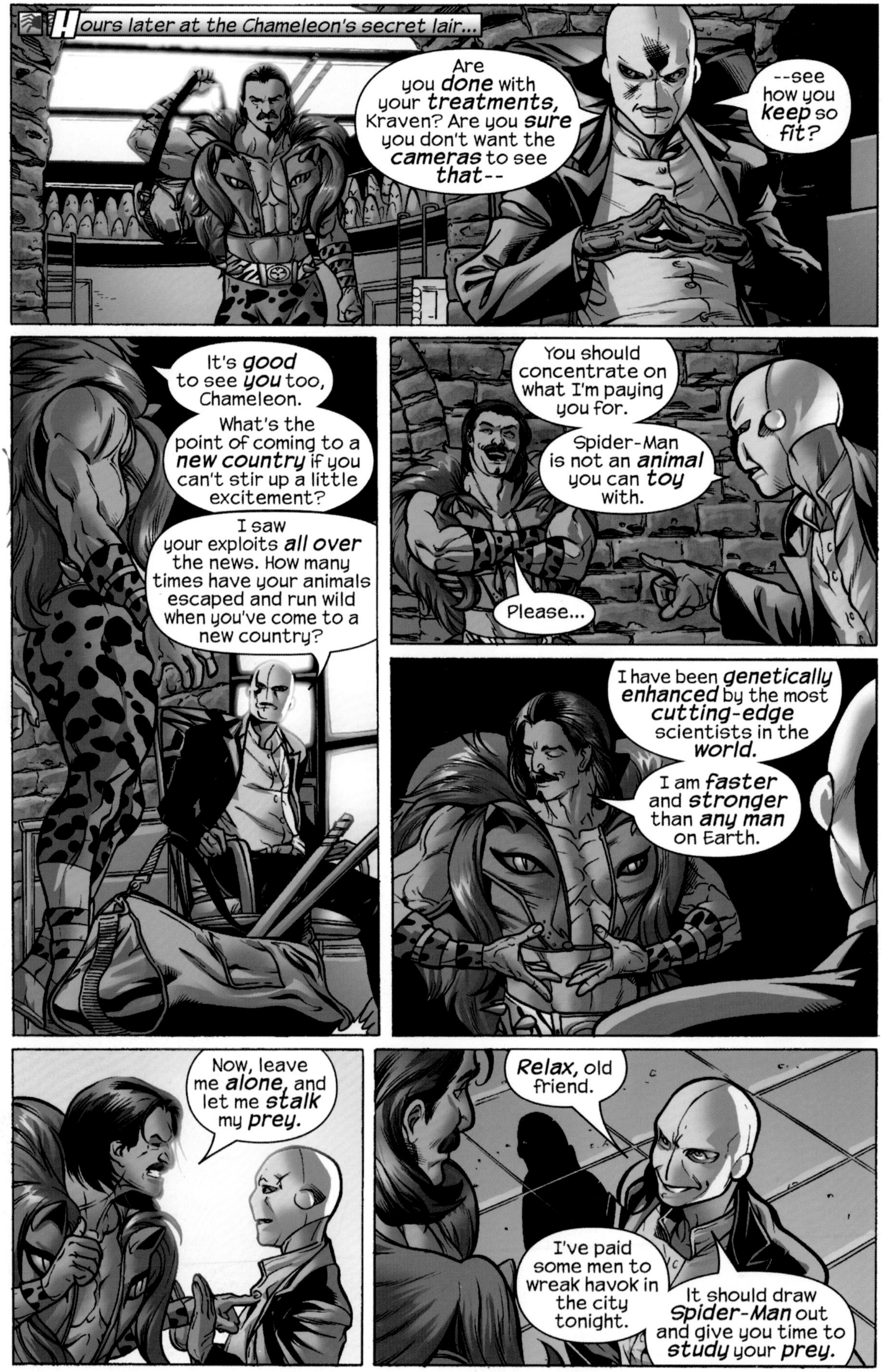
Hours later at the Chameleon's secret lair...
Are you done with your treatments, Kraven? Are you sure you don't want the cameras to see that--
--see how you keep so fit?
It's good to see you too, Chameleon.
What's the point of coming to a new country if you can't stir up a little excitement?
I saw your exploits all over the news. How many times have your animals escaped and run wild when you've come to a new country?
You should concentrate on what I'm paying you for.
Spider-Man is not an animal you can toy with.
Please...
I have been genetically enhanced by the most cutting-edge scientists in the world.
I am faster and stronger than any man on Earth.
Now, leave me alone, and let me stalk my prey.
Relax, old friend.
I've paid some men to wreak havok in the city tonight.
It should draw Spider-Man out and give you time to study your prey.

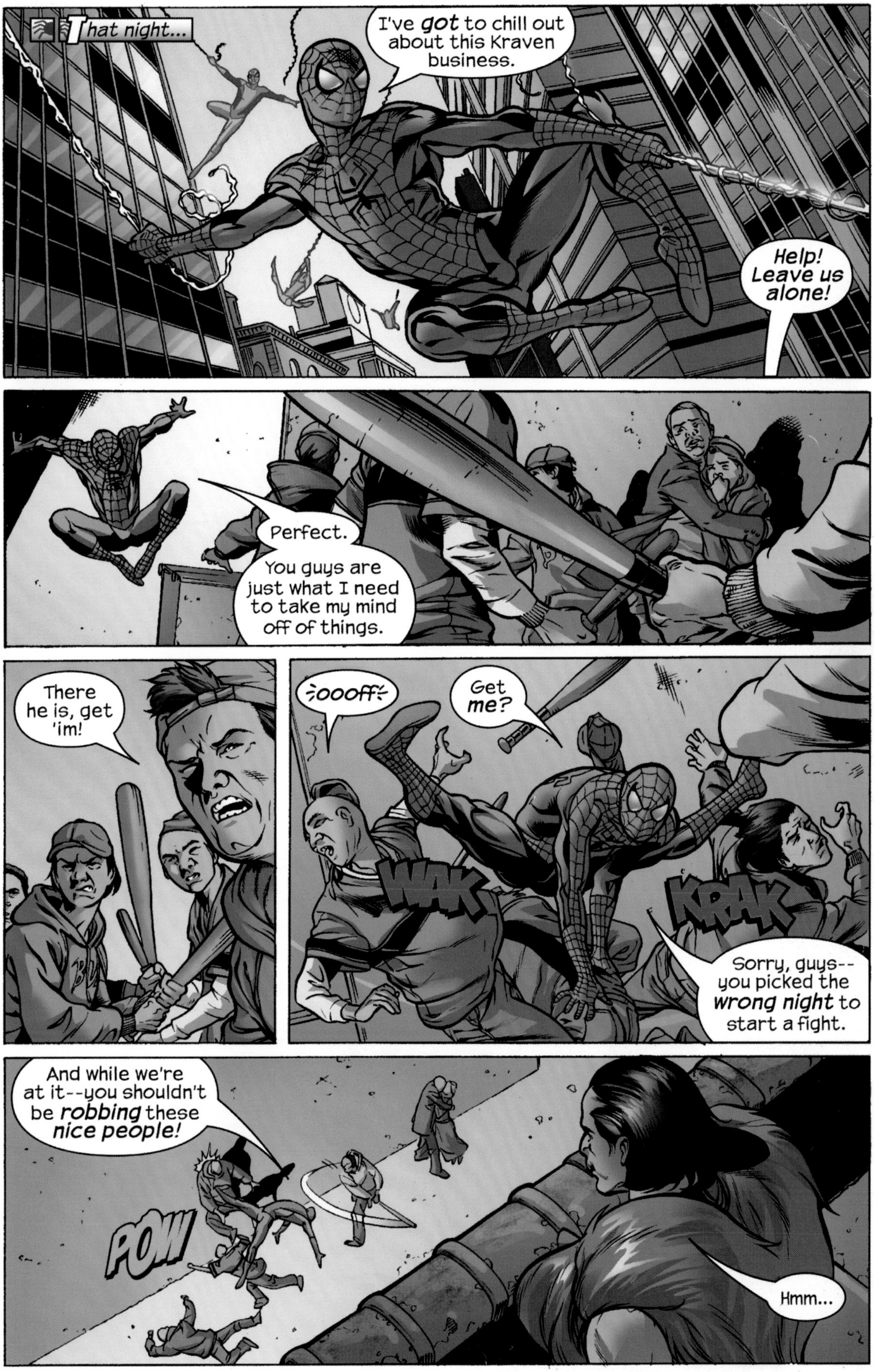
That night...
I've got to chill out about this Kraven business.
Help! Leave us alone!
Perfect.
You guys are just what I need to take my mind off of things.
There he is, get 'im!
oooff
Get me?
WAK
KRAK
Sorry, guys-- you picked the wrong night to start a fight.
And while we're at it--you shouldn't be robbing these nice people!
POW
Hmm...

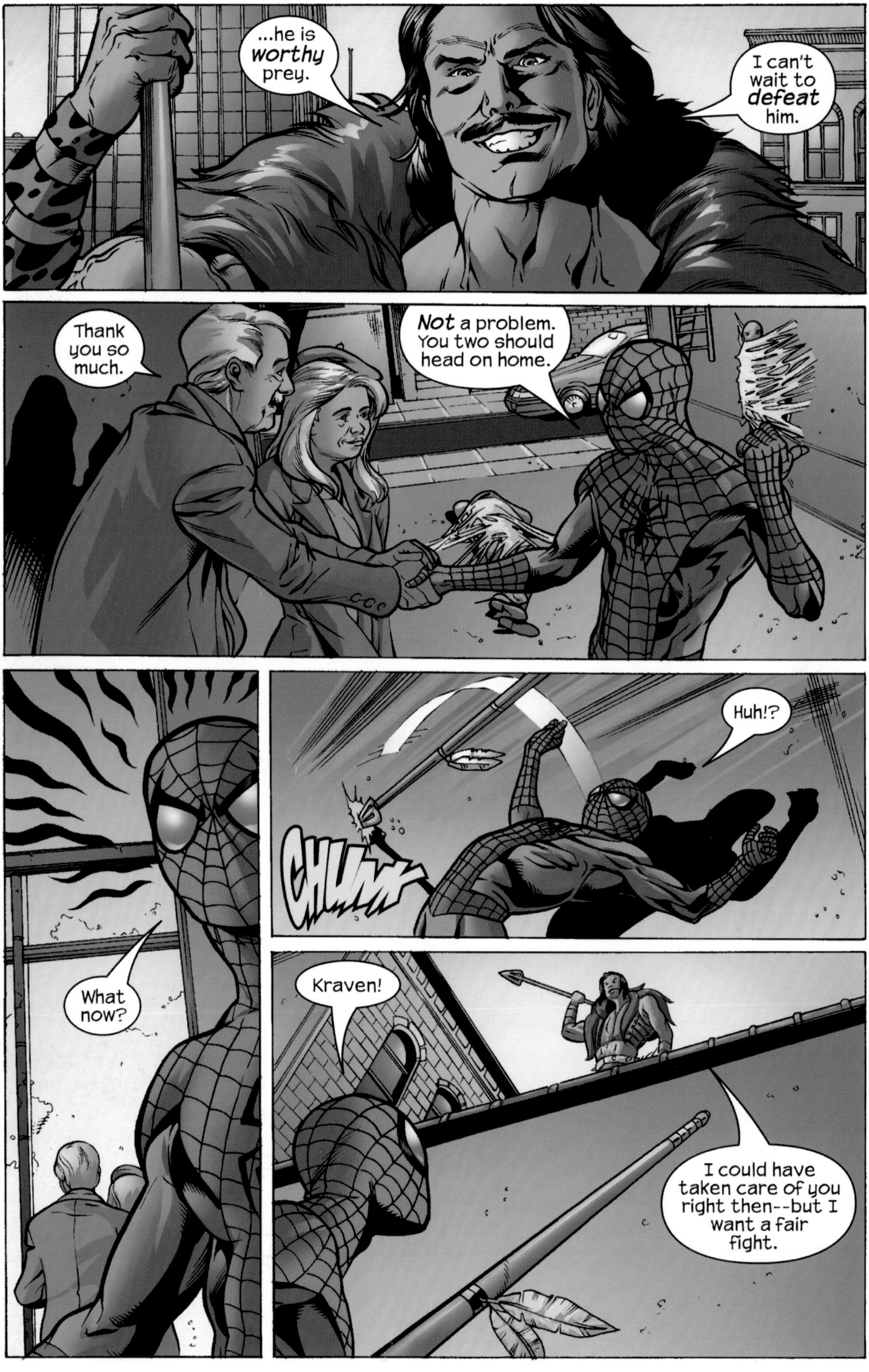
...he is worthy prey.
I can't wait to defeat him.
Thank you so much.
Not a problem. You two should head on home.
What now?
Huh!?
CHUNK
Kraven!
I could have taken care of you right then--but I want a fair fight.

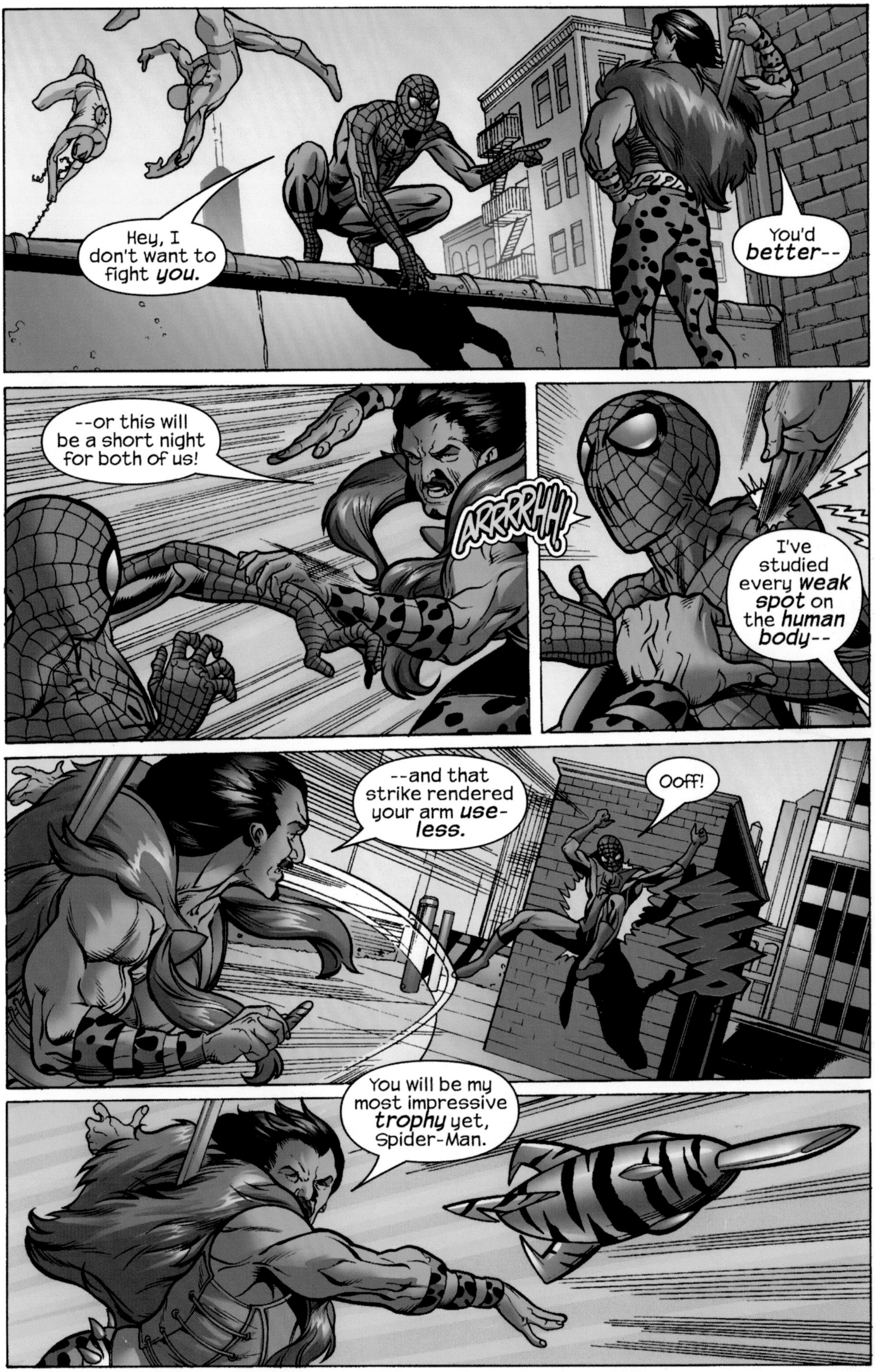
Hey, I don't want to fight *you.*
You'd *better*--
--or this will be a short night for both of us!
ARRRRHH!
I've studied every *weak spot* on the *human body*--
--and that strike rendered your arm *use-less.*
Ooff!
You will be my most impressive *trophy* yet, Spider-Man.

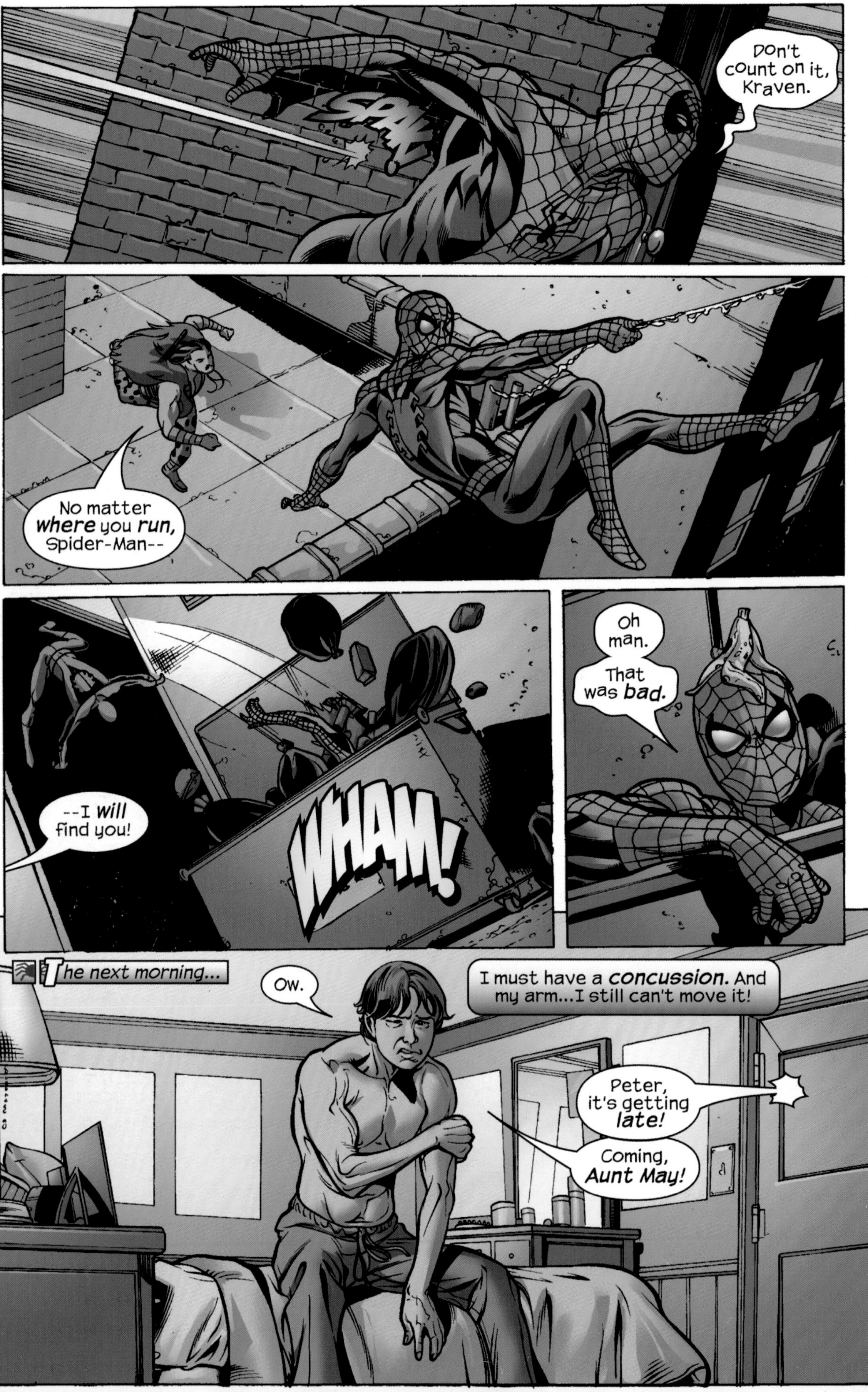

SPAK
Don't count on it, Kraven.
No matter where you run, Spider-Man--
--I will find you!
WHAM!
Oh man.
That was bad.
The next morning...
Ow.
I must have a concussion. And my arm...I still can't move it!
Peter, it's getting late!
Coming, Aunt May!

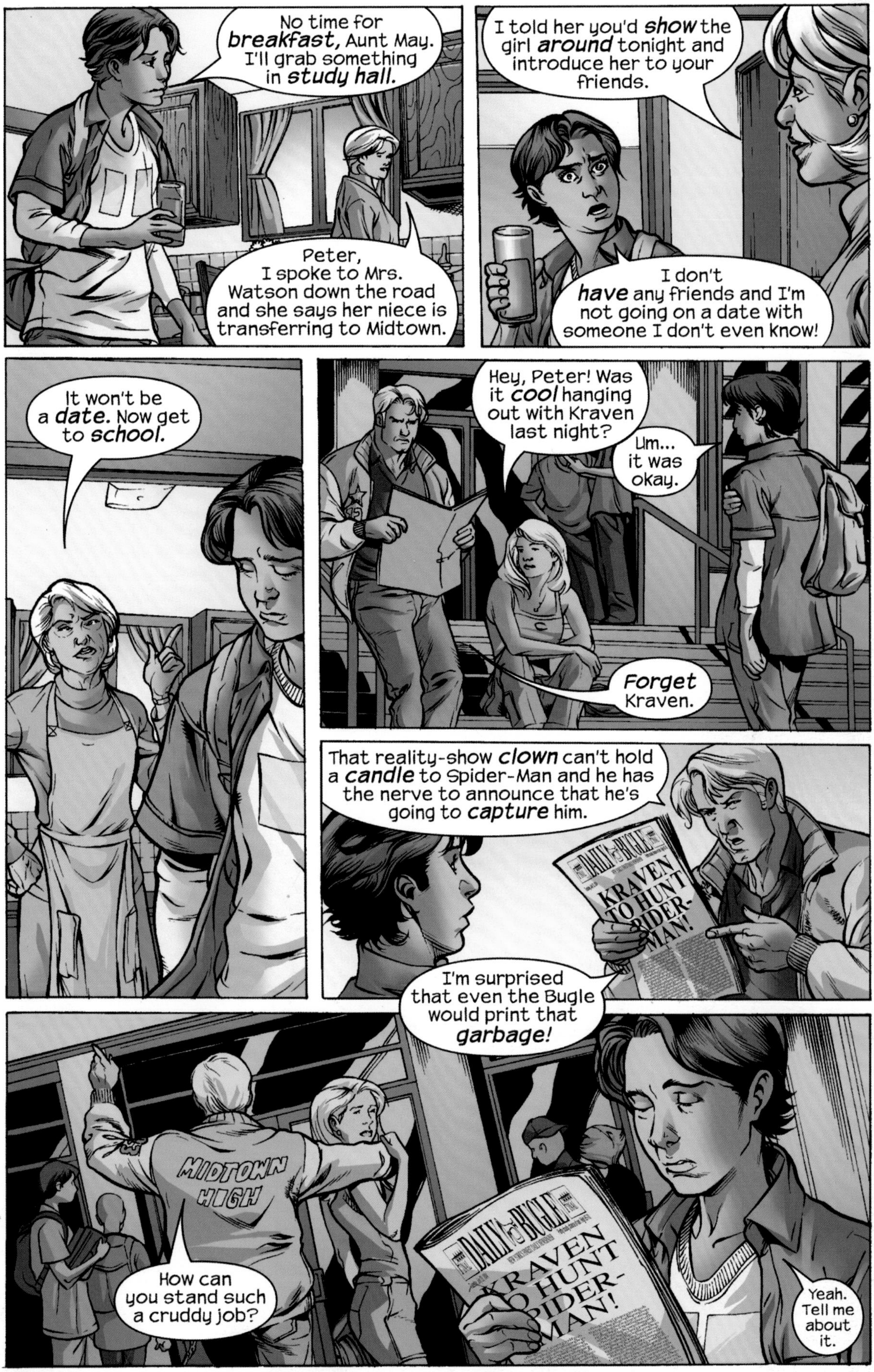
No time for breakfast, Aunt May. I'll grab something in study hall.
Peter, I spoke to Mrs. Watson down the road and she says her niece is transferring to Midtown.
I told her you'd show the girl around tonight and introduce her to your friends.
I don't have any friends and I'm not going on a date with someone I don't even know!
It won't be a date. Now get to school.
Hey, Peter! Was it cool hanging out with Kraven last night?
Um... it was okay.
Forget Kraven.
That reality-show clown can't hold a candle to Spider-Man and he has the nerve to announce that he's going to capture him.
KRAVEN TO HUNT
I'm surprised that even the Bugle would print that garbage!
MIDTOWN HIGH
How can you stand such a cruddy job?
DAILY BUGLE
KRAVEN
Yeah. Tell me about it.

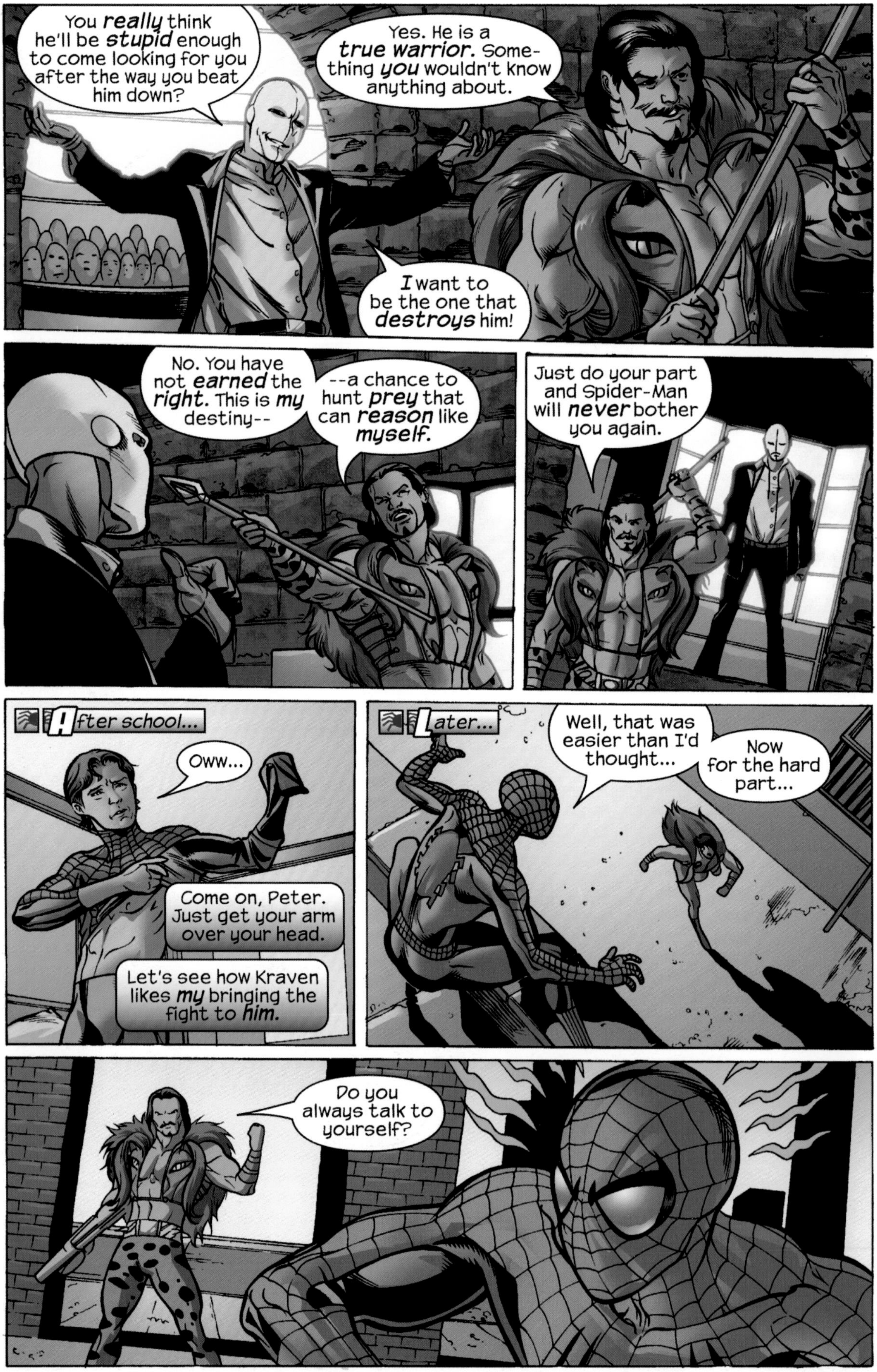
You really think he'll be stupid enough to come looking for you after the way you beat him down?
Yes. He is a true warrior. Something you wouldn't know anything about.
I want to be the one that destroys him!
No. You have not earned the right. This is my destiny--
--a chance to hunt prey that can reason like myself.
Just do your part and Spider-Man will never bother you again.
After school...
Oww...
Come on, Peter. Just get your arm over your head.
Let's see how Kraven likes my bringing the fight to him.
Later...
Well, that was easier than I'd thought...
Now for the hard part...
Do you always talk to yourself?

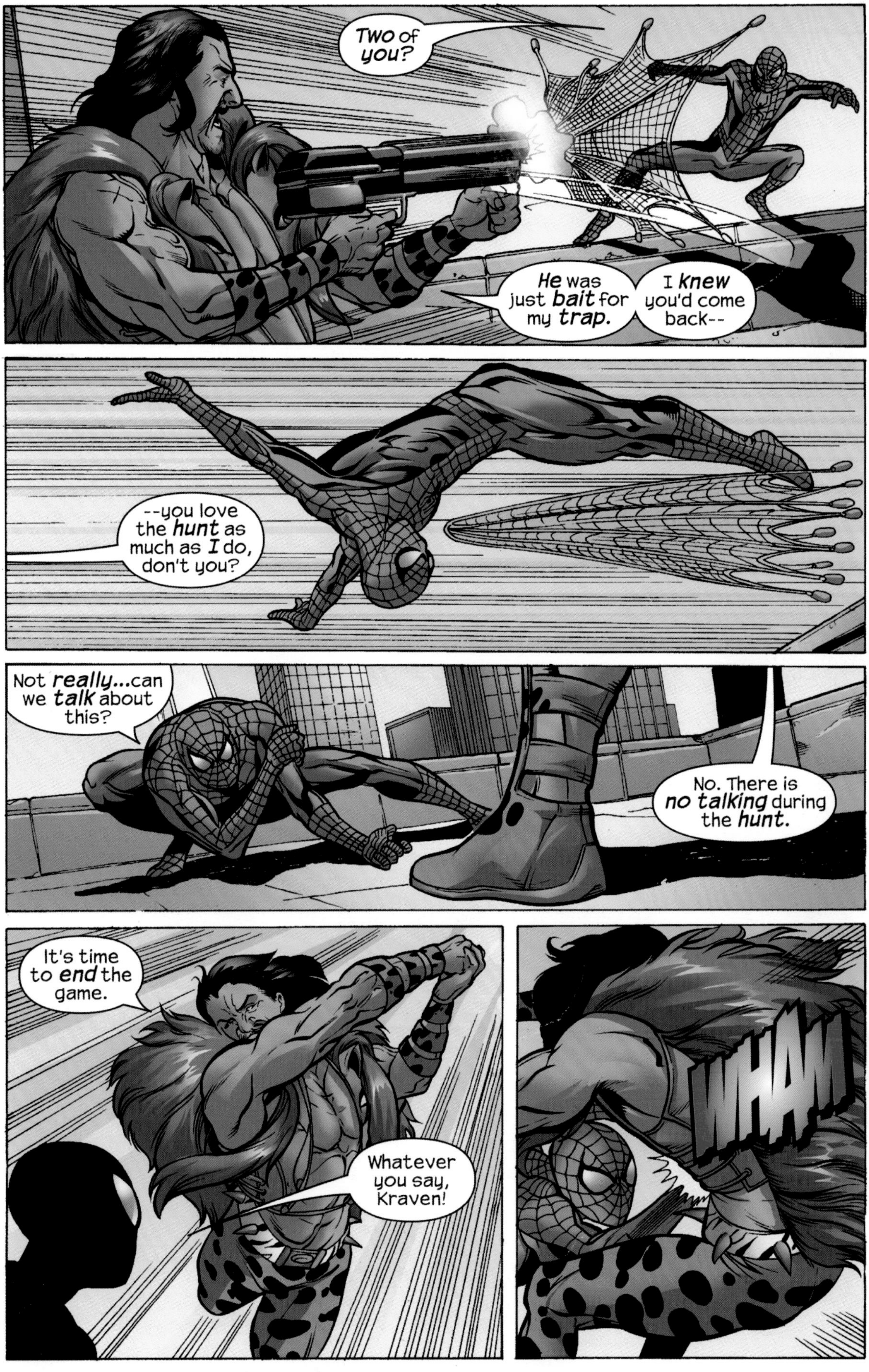

Two of you?
He was just bait for my trap.
I knew you'd come back--
--you love the hunt as much as I do, don't you?
Not really...can we talk about this?
No. There is no talking during the hunt.
It's time to end the game.
Whatever you say, Kraven!
WHAM

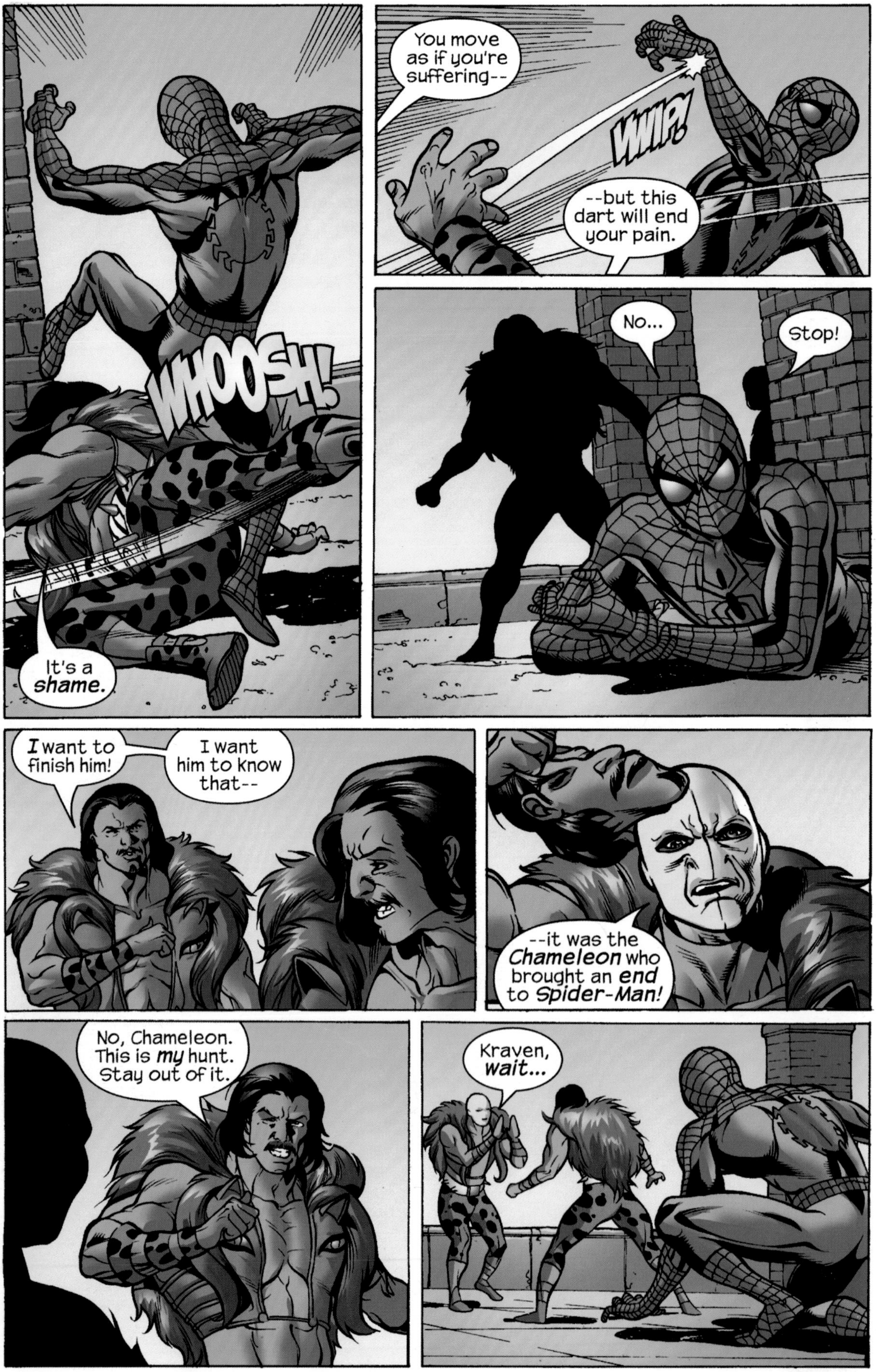
WHOOSH!
It's a *shame.*
You move as if you're suffering--
WWIP!
--but this dart will end your pain.
No...
Stop!
I want to finish him!
I want him to know that--
--it was the *Chameleon* who brought an *end* to *Spider-Man!*
No, Chameleon. This is *my* hunt. Stay out of it.
Kraven, *wait...*

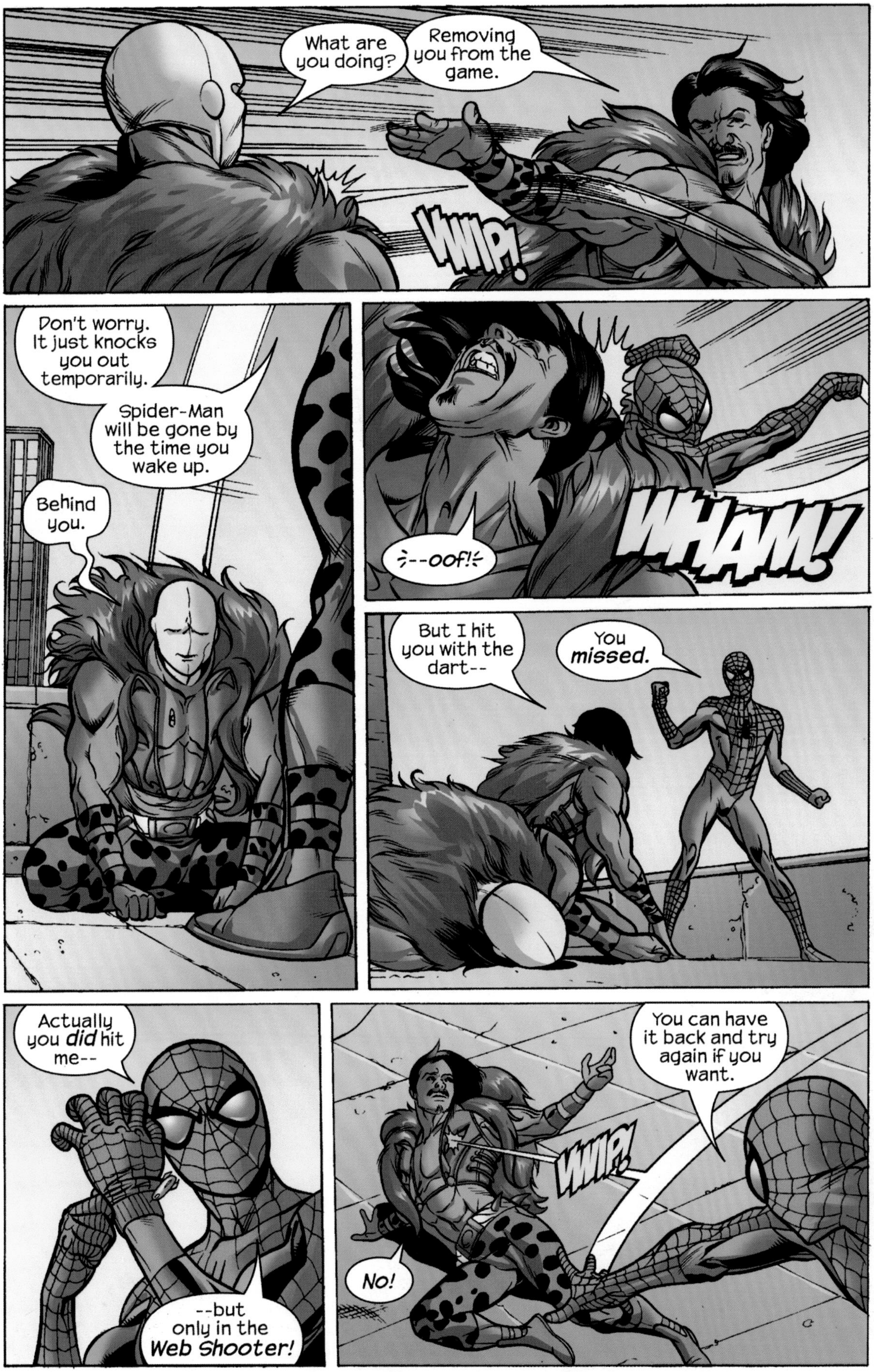
What are you doing?
Removing you from the game.
WWIP!
Don't worry. It just knocks you out temporarily.
Spider-Man will be gone by the time you wake up.
Behind you.
WHAM!
--oof!
But I hit you with the dart--
You missed.
Actually you did hit me--
--but only in the Web Shooter!
You can have it back and try again if you want.
WWIP!
No!

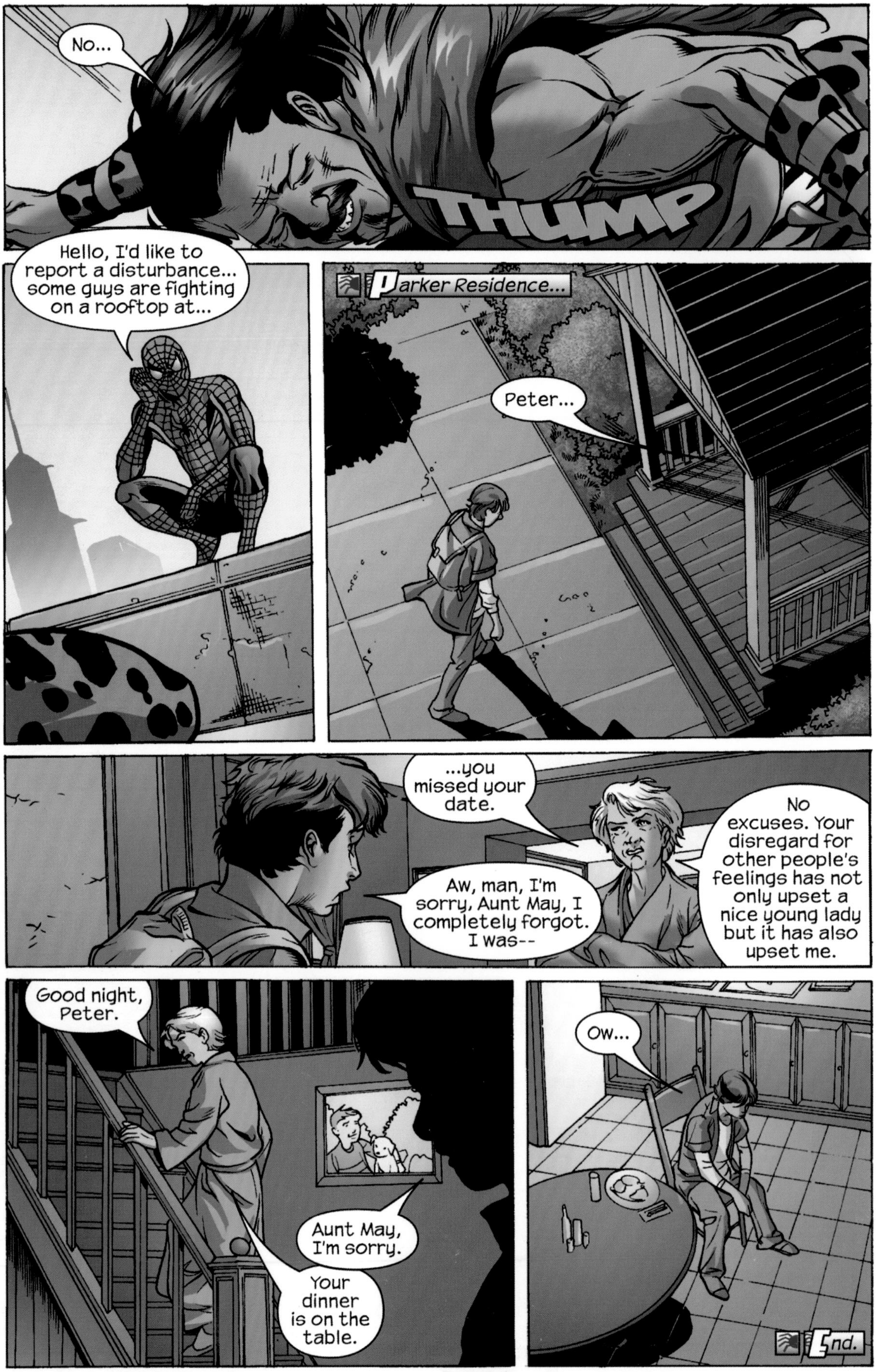
No...
THUMP
Hello, I'd like to report a disturbance... some guys are fighting on a rooftop at...
Parker Residence...
Peter...
...you missed your date.
Aw, man, I'm sorry, Aunt May, I completely forgot. I was--
No excuses. Your disregard for other people's feelings has not only upset a nice young lady but it has also upset me.
Good night, Peter.
Aunt May, I'm sorry.
Your dinner is on the table.
Ow...
End.